The Shimmering Ciphe

Raja Sharma

www.draft2digital.com

Copyright

Copyright@2023 Raja Sharma

Published by: Education Corner

Draft2digital Edition

Table of Contents

Preface

In the depths of an enigmatic world lies a tale of love that transcends boundaries and defies expectations. Welcome to "The Shimmering Cipher: Love Uncharted," a captivating journey that will take you on an emotional rollercoaster through the intricacies of life, love, and the unforeseen connections that fate weaves.

Within these pages, you will meet Sunayana and Morgan, two souls brought together by the twists of destiny. Sunayana, a young woman from India pursuing her dreams in the land of opportunities, and Morgan, a self-made man with a past shrouded in mystery, find themselves unexpectedly entangled in a bond that knows no boundaries.

As their paths intertwine, they are faced with trials and tribulations, challenging societal norms and confronting their deepest fears. Their story unfolds against the backdrop of a cultural clash, where love is questioned, and sacrifices are made in the name of acceptance.

The journey of Sunayana and Morgan is not just a tale of romance but an exploration of resilience, determination, and the pursuit of dreams. It will make you question the very essence of love and the courage it takes to follow your heart, no matter the obstacles in your way.

"The Shimmering Cipher: Love Uncharted" is a testament to the power of love, the strength of the human spirit, and the beauty of embracing the unknown. Join us as we embark on this extraordinary expedition of emotions, where love blooms in the most unexpected places and the heart finds solace in the uncharted territories of life.

Open the first page and let the secrets of "The Shimmering Cipher" unravel before your eyes, leaving you spellbound and eager to unearth every twist and turn that awaits. The journey begins, and the adventure of a lifetime awaits you.

Chapter 1

At College

On a bright morning, the road bustled with its customary busy traffic. For the last fifteen minutes, Sunayana had been stationed at the curb, attempting to flag down taxis. However, most taxis whizzed by, already occupied with passengers. Her urgency to secure a cab grew with each passing moment.

As a cab approached her, she locked her gaze on it and lifted her hand, successfully halting the vehicle with a screech of its tires. Behind the wheel sat a handsome American taxi driver. As he rolled down the window, a warm smile graced his features, causing Sunayana to collect herself and regain her composure.

With a courteous tone, the driver inquired, "Where would you like to go, Miss?"

Providing the name of her college, Sunayana settled into the back seat. To her surprise, she intended to offer directions, but the driver was already well-acquainted with the route to her college.

"You need not worry, Miss. I know the place well. Just let me know the name of your department, and we'll get you there promptly," the driver reassured her with politeness.

Sunayana conveyed the name of her department, feeling a sense of relief washing over her. She was glad that she would reach her destination on time.

After approximately twenty-five minutes, the taxi pulled up in front of Sunayana's department. The driver promptly stepped out, opening the door for her.

As she prepared to leave, the driver's friendly demeanor continued. "May I take the liberty to ask you when will your class be over, miss? If you wish, I'd be more than happy to return to pick you up," he offered graciously, accompanied by a bright smile.

"Thank you for the kind offer, but I'll manage on my own," Sunayana replied, returning his warm smile.

"Miss, I feel obliged to inform you that the location where you hired my cab is not favored by taxi drivers in the evening. Furthermore, there are no evening buses available to take you there. The road repair work has resulted in one-way traffic during that time, making it quite challenging to reach your destination," the cab driver earnestly attempted to explain the situation to Sunayana.

Sunayana graciously smiled and responded, "Thank you so much for your concern. I'm accustomed to overcoming challenges, and I'll manage just fine. Nonetheless, I truly appreciate your kind offer."

As she prepared to leave, the cab driver insisted, "Regardless, please keep my card with you, just in case you need a cab in the future." He gently placed a card in her hand before bidding her farewell.

Sunayana opened her purse and handed the driver the fare. After the transaction was completed, she carefully placed his card inside her purse for safekeeping. As the cab driver started his vehicle and drove away, Sunayana watched him depart, feeling grateful for the assistance he had provided.

For a brief moment, Sunayana considered discarding the card, but upon second thought, she gazed at it once more and decided to retain it. The name 'Morgan Shaw' and the associated phone number were clearly visible on the card, intriguing her curiosity. She carefully placed it back into her purse, acknowledging that it might come in handy at some point in the future.

Chapter 2

New Ambience

Just a week prior, Sunayana had arrived in the United States. Her father's friend's son, named Raman, resided in that town, and it was decided that Sunayana would live with Raman and his family during her stay.

During her initial days at Raman's place, Sunayana had called her parents, who were delighted to learn that she had found Raman and his family to be exceptionally warm and amiable. Their hearts were put at ease by this news.

As the days passed, Sunayana became an integral part of their household, feeling like a cherished family member. Raman, Neelima, and their little daughter, Meeta, treated her with utmost courtesy and kindness, earning Sunayana's admiration and respect. Meeta, in particular, was thrilled to have found a new playmate in Sunayana, adding to her happiness in the house.

After a week had passed, Sunayana approached Raman with a request to help her find an apartment. Although he was hesitant about her staying elsewhere, he understood her need for privacy as a young girl. With a considerate heart, Raman managed to locate an apartment situated close to his own house, ensuring that Sunayana would have her own space while remaining nearby.

Upon settling into her own apartment, Sunayana came to a profound realization - she had seamlessly integrated into the fabric of that society. The once intimidating big city no longer felt like an alien place to her. Instead, she embraced a sense of belonging, no longer considering herself a stranger.

The warmth and acceptance shown by Raman, Neelima, Meeta, and the people around her had woven her into the social tapestry of the city, making her feel right at home.

Within a few days of living independently, Sunayana soon recognized the challenges of navigating America without a car. Realizing the importance of mobility, she made the decision to enroll in a driving school to acquire her driving skills.

During this period of learning, Raman kindly extended his support by dropping her off at college and picking her up after school for about a week. His continued assistance made Sunayana's transition into life with a car much smoother and more manageable.

Today, feeling a sense of independence and determination, Sunayana opted to take a taxi to her college. She realized she was no longer a child and desired to explore the world on her terms. This decision brought her immense satisfaction and contentment.

Raman had informed her about a convenient bus route that could take her to and from her college. However, he also assured her that in case she missed the bus, she could always rely on taking a cab as a backup plan. This information provided Sunayana with a safety net, giving her the confidence to embrace her newfound freedom and self-reliance.

This morning, as Sunayana prepared to lock the door of her apartment, she suddenly realized that she had forgotten to place the key in her purse. Searching for the key took nearly half an hour, causing her to miss her bus. Despite the inconvenience, she considered herself fortunate as she managed to find a taxi nearby, allowing her to reach her college on time despite the initial setback.

Sunayana had ventured to the United States with the purpose of pursuing her M.B.A. She found herself enamored with her college, especially her department, where the lectures delivered by her professors left a lasting impression on her. The intellectual stimulation and knowledge imparted in these classes deeply impressed her.

Furthermore, Sunayana was delighted to discover that she was not the only foreign student in her class. Several other international students, like her, added to the diversity and global perspective of the learning environment, making her educational experience even more enriching.

Within a short span, Sunayana developed several close friendships with non-American students, who warmly accepted her into their circle. She felt incredibly at ease with her friends, appreciating the absence of bias or racial discrimination in her college environment.

The majority of her classmates displayed a strong dedication to their studies, approaching their academic pursuits with diligence and seriousness. It was only natural, given that they had all come to America with dreams to fulfill, and success hinged on their hard work and commitment to excel.

The atmosphere in her college, especially during class discussions, delighted Sunayana. The friendly and amicable ambiance fostered an ideal setting for productive learning and meaningful interactions. She was content with her decision to come to America, recognizing that it had been the right choice to embark on this academic journey and enrich her life in so many ways.

Upon arriving at her class, Sunayana attentively listened to Professor Morrison's lecture. Impressed by his insights, he mentioned some valuable books that piqued her interest.

Eager to explore those recommended books, Sunayana headed to the library after class. However, her enthusiasm was curtailed when she discovered that she couldn't borrow any books without a library card. Instead, she selected one of the books and settled into a quiet corner, engrossed in its contents.

Hours passed by unnoticed as Sunayana immersed herself in the captivating read. It was only when she finally emerged from the book's world that she realized the daylight had dimmed into darkness. In a hurry, she made her way to the bus stand, but her hopes were dashed when she found out that the last bus had already departed.

Sunayana, feeling a bit worried about the situation, approached a group of college boys who were waiting for a different bus. Politely, she inquired if they knew of any available buses or taxis that could take her back to her apartment.

One of the boys responded similarly to the taxi driver from earlier, "I'm afraid there are no buses or taxis at this hour. Your best bet would be to call a cab if you have the number."

Sunayana recollected the card given to her by Morgan in the morning. With a glimmer of hope, she dialed his number and introduced herself, "Hello, Morgan. I'm Sunayana. You dropped me off at my college this morning. Do you remember? I'm in need of a ride. Would you be able to come and pick me up?"

Morgan's reassuring response brought immense relief to Sunayana. "Thank you so much; I'll wait at the bus stand," she replied before Morgan disconnected the call.

As she stood alone at the bus stand, Sunayana's usually unwavering confidence seemed to waver a bit. The absence of the young boys who had been there earlier made her feel somewhat uneasy. However, after about twenty minutes of anticipation, she spotted a yellow cab approaching from a distance, and a wave of relief washed over her.

When Morgan finally arrived to pick her up, Sunayana expressed her gratitude and thanked him for coming to her aid. The sense of comfort and security she felt in that moment reaffirmed her faith in the kindness of people, leaving her grateful for the assistance she had received.

Sunayana settled into the yellow cab, appreciative of Morgan's swift arrival. Curious about how he managed to reach so quickly, she voiced her question, "Thank you very much, but how did you make it here so fast?"

Morgan's warm smile remained as he explained, "I work part-time in the computer department. When I received your call, I realized that you might be in need of help, so I immediately set off to pick you up."

Sunayana was pleasantly taken aback by Morgan's thoughtful gesture. "That's really kind of you," she replied. Then, her curiosity piqued, she asked, "By the way, what do you do in the computer department?"

As the cab journeyed on, Morgan shared his aspirations for a better job, acknowledging the significance of computers in today's world. When Sunayana inquired about his qualifications, Morgan's response revealed a hint of sadness as he explained that he didn't have the same familial support she enjoyed. He had to work hard to pursue his studies independently.

Sunayana, deeply moved by his determination and resilience, sought to comfort him. "Only a few people possess the courage to progress through their own efforts, and you are one of them," she said warmly, offering her support and encouragement.

Grateful for her kind words, Morgan responded in Hindi, "Thank you, your inspiring words give me a lot of encouragement." In that moment, a sense of connection and understanding seemed to bridge the gap between them, fostering a meaningful exchange that touched both their hearts.

Sunayana was genuinely amazed by Morgan's interest in Hindi. Her curiosity led her to inquire further, "Do you speak Hindi?"

With a shy yet determined smile, Morgan replied, "I am learning Hindi. I haven't mastered it yet, but I truly believe that one day I'll be able to speak it fluently."

Intrigued, Sunayana couldn't help but ask, "Why do you want to study Hindi?"

Morgan's response carried a strong sense of purpose, "My father spent several years in India, and I've heard so much about the country from him. It has always fascinated me. I'm determined to visit India one day." His conviction in this dream was evident in his words, leaving Sunayana deeply impressed by his passion for learning and his desire to explore new cultures.

Sunayana found herself increasingly engaged in the conversation. "You're right," she replied thoughtfully, "English is widely spoken in India, and you can get by without knowing Hindi. But why do you think learning Hindi is essential?"

Morgan's response held a deep sense of conviction, "Language is a bridge that connects people. While it may not be necessary to know Hindi, I believe that learning it will help me connect with the culture and the people on a deeper level. Just like in this country, where knowledge of English is highly valued, I think it's important to show respect and appreciation for the language of the place I wish to visit."

Sunayana admired Morgan's serious approach to understanding and respecting different cultures. His determination to embrace a new language as a means of connecting with others left a profound impression on her, further strengthening the bond between them during the cab ride.

Sunayana was deeply moved by the realization that Morgan was not just an ordinary cab driver. He possessed a drive and ambition that surpassed the norm, aspiring for something greater than average.

With a warm smile, Sunayana responded, "No, it's genuinely wonderful to know that you're interested in learning the language of my country."

Their eyes met through the rear-view mirror, creating an unspoken connection. Sunayana felt a sudden rush of emotions and shyly averted her gaze.

Morgan, ever the considerate one, made an offer to help. "If you agree, I can drive you to your college in my taxi every day," he suggested.

While appreciative of his offer, Sunayana politely declined, "Thank you, Morgan, but I can't afford to travel by taxi every day. However, if I ever need a ride, I'll definitely give you a call."

Their exchange highlighted the genuine bond they had formed during the cab ride, leaving Sunayana with a newfound respect and admiration for Morgan's determination and kind-heartedness.

Morgan's expectation shone on his face as he made a generous offer, "You can pay me the fare you would pay for bus travel. I've read 'Ramayana' and 'Gita' in English, and now I'm eager to read them in Hindi. Would you be able to spare some time to help me read these holy books?"

Sunayana was delighted that he wanted to explore their scriptures and was ready to help.

However, she couldn't accept his money for teaching him Hindi. She chuckled warmly, "I'm glad you want to read our scriptures, but I can't charge you for teaching you Hindi. Let me pay you the bus fare; that way, I can contribute a little."

Morgan, ever respectful, insisted, "My father was right about Indians using their heart, and that's what makes you all so sentimental. We Americans are quite practical. Please accept my condition. I won't lose anything; in fact, I'll benefit from it."

Sunayana recognized Morgan's sincerity and his eagerness to learn, appreciating his words. She agreed, touched by his humility and eagerness to embrace a new language and culture. The exchange further solidified their newfound friendship and mutual respect.

Sunayana appreciated Morgan's determination and his genuine willingness to learn. She took a moment to consider his offer, realizing the sincerity in his words and the earnestness of his desire to explore Indian scriptures through Hindi.

After contemplating for a while, Morgan broke the silence, "What time do you have your class tomorrow? Be ready tomorrow. Now it's my responsibility to take you to your college and bring you back to your apartment. Please accept my respect."

Sunayana was deeply moved by his gesture and accepted graciously, "All right, I will be ready at 8:00 am tomorrow. I plan to read some books in the library."

"Thank you! I'll be there right on time," replied Morgan with enthusiasm, eager to fulfill his newfound responsibility and build on the bond they had established. As their conversation ended, both of them felt a sense of connection and companionship that had started with a simple taxi ride and evolved into something far more meaningful.

Chapter 3

Life Moves On

Back in her apartment, Sunayana found herself deep in thought, reflecting on the recent events. She questioned whether it had been appropriate to share so much personal information with a stranger like the taxi driver, Morgan. In India, she would have been more cautious and wary of such interactions.

She puzzled over her decision to accept Morgan's condition, allowing him to pay the fare in exchange for Hindi lessons. Although she recognized his intelligence and qualifications, she couldn't fully comprehend her own response. Seeking guidance, she decided to discuss the matter with Raman and his wife, Neelima, seeking their perspective.

In an attempt to relax her mind, Sunayana picked up a novel and read a few pages before eventually drifting off to sleep. The whirlwind of emotions and thoughts had taken a toll on her, leaving her to rest and gather her thoughts before seeking counsel from her newfound friends.

The next morning, Sunayana was taken aback by the unexpected doorbell ringing, as she had rarely received visitors, especially at such an early hour.

Opening the door, she was pleasantly surprised to find Morgan standing there, greeting her with a warm "Namaste!" His broad and polite smile left a positive impression on Sunayana.

Morgan informed her that he was waiting near his cab. Sunayana, feeling comfortable around him, suggested, "All right, I'll be there soon. Is it too late to offer you a cup of tea?"

Polite and considerate as ever, Morgan replied, "I just had coffee. You can take your time and then come down. There's no hurry at all." With that, he turned and left Sunayana's doorstep, respecting her space and giving her the time she needed.

His demeanor only reinforced the respect and admiration Sunayana had developed for him, making her feel even more grateful for their growing friendship.

She swiftly finished her tea, gathered her belongings, locked her apartment, and made her way down the stairs.

In no time, she found herself standing before the waiting cab. Morgan, ever considerate, left his driving seat and hurriedly came to open the back door for her, demonstrating his courtesy and attentiveness once again. Sunayana appreciated his thoughtfulness and smiled, appreciating the respect he showed her.

Sunayana felt a growing comfort and familiarity with Morgan, and her curiosity got the better of her. She hesitated slightly before suggesting, "What do you say if I sit on the front seat beside you?"

Morgan's face lit up with enthusiasm, and he replied, "Why not? Of course, it'll be easier for us to converse. I'll make an effort to speak in Hindi with you. Please feel free to correct me if I make any mistakes." He kindly opened the front door for her, allowing her to take the seat beside him.

As they embarked on their journey, Sunayana's curiosity got the better of her, and she couldn't resist asking, "I'm curious, Morgan. Why are you in such a hurry to learn Hindi? What's the reason behind your interest in our language?"

As Morgan revealed his heartfelt reason for learning Hindi, Sunayana was deeply moved. He spoke with sincerity about his desire to visit India and pay his respects at his grandmother's grave by fulfilling the promise he had made to his grandfather before his passing.

Sunayana's eyes shone with admiration and respect for Morgan's strong bond with his family and his deep sense of sentiment. She expressed her feelings, saying, "I'm truly impressed by your respect and love for your grandmother and grandfather. It's heartwarming to see such sentiments in a modern American like you."

However, Sunayana's joy was momentarily overshadowed as she realized she might have made a hasty assumption about Americans lacking emotions. She quickly apologized, "I'm sorry, I didn't mean to imply that. I shouldn't have said that." She felt a sense of regret for her unintentional mistake and resolved to be more thoughtful with her words in the future.

As they continued their conversation, Morgan further elaborated on his reasons for wanting to take a break and spend some time away from his country. He had been working and studying for many years, and now he felt the need for a change. He chose India as his destination, emphasizing that it was the world's largest democracy.

Sunayana appreciated Morgan's unique perspective and said, "You are different from other Americans. I mean, you understand life better than them."

Morgan laughed at the compliment and replied, "I am flattered! Thank you for saying that. All right, here we are. Your college! Give me a ring in the evening after your class, and I will be here to pick you up in no time."

Sunayana thanked him, expressing her gratitude for his dependable assistance. She stepped out of the cab, feeling fortunate to have met someone like Morgan, who not only understood the value of sentiments and relationships but also possessed a curiosity and appreciation for different cultures. As she entered her college, she looked forward to the evening when she could continue their conversation and learn more about Morgan's intriguing journey and his dream to visit India.

In the evening, as promised, Morgan arrived on time. They sat in his cab and engaged in a lively conversation in Hindi for about half an hour. Morgan made an earnest effort to communicate, occasionally switching to English when he encountered difficulties.

Sunayana listened attentively and patiently corrected him whenever necessary. After this brief session, she was impressed by his progress, realizing that within a month, he would likely be able to communicate effectively enough to navigate freely in India.

As their language practice concluded, Sunayana requested Morgan to drop her off at her uncle's house, which happened to be right behind her apartment. Morgan readily agreed and assured her that he would be ready to pick her up the next morning as well.

Outside Raman's house, Sunayana bid farewell to Morgan and started walking toward the front door, feeling content and grateful for the delightful and productive time they had spent together. She couldn't help but look forward to the journey of helping Morgan learn Hindi and the shared excitement of his upcoming visit to India.

Meeta warmly embraced Sunayana, expressing how much she missed her presence, "Without you, our house seems deserted. Nothing feels quite as pleasant."

With a beaming smile, Sunayana reassured Meeta, "Don't worry, I live just a few yards away. You can call me anytime, or feel free to come to my apartment."

After bolting the door from inside, Meeta led Sunayana to the drawing room, where they settled comfortably. Meeta inquired about Sunayana's college experience and asked if there were any transportation issues. Raman, curious as well, suggested that he could come to pick her up in the evenings.

Sunayana happily shared, "No, everything is going smoothly. I've actually made a friend."

Raman's surprise was evident as he exclaimed, "What? You've made a friend in just two weeks!"

Sunayana explained with a chuckle, "Well, he's a taxi driver. He picks me up every morning and drops me off every evening." She recounted the heartwarming story of her friendship with Morgan, highlighting his eagerness to learn Hindi and his dream of visiting India to fulfill his promise to his grandfather. Both Meeta and Raman listened attentively, touched by the unexpected bond that had blossomed in such a short time.

Sunayana shared every detail of her encounters with Morgan and the arrangement they had made for language practice. As she spoke, Raman's serious demeanor caught her attention. He remarked, "He doesn't seem like an ordinary cab driver; he appears to be quite intelligent. I have a feeling he drives a taxi only part-time."

Sunayana agreed, saying, "It's possible. He did mention that education is expensive here, and driving a taxi helps him finance his studies."

Raman seemed intrigued by Morgan and resolved, "All right, when I have some free time, I'll try to find out more about this Morgan of yours."

As the conversation continued, Meeta listened attentively, equally curious about Sunayana's newfound friend. They both appreciated Morgan's dedication to learning Hindi and admired his ambition to explore India. Sunayana was grateful for their interest and support, feeling fortunate to have such caring relatives who were always there for her.

The evening spent with Meeta and Raman was delightful for Sunayana. They shared a delicious dinner together before going out for a leisurely walk. The pleasant weather added to their enjoyment as they stopped by a nearby store for ice cream.

After a fulfilling and enjoyable time, Sunayana returned to her apartment late in the evening, feeling content and happy. The warmth of family and the cherished moments shared with her loved ones had filled her heart with joy.

As the morning sunlight filtered into her room, Sunayana opened her eyes and was greeted by a pleasant weather. The gentle breeze carried the fragrance of the garden located just behind her building, and she felt invigorated by the fresh air flowing into her room.

Her attention was drawn to a wooden bench in the garden, not far from her window. To her surprise, she spotted Morgan sitting on that bench with a laptop computer on his lap. His fingers moved swiftly across the keyboard, engrossed in whatever task he was working on.

Sunayana observed more carefully to confirm that it was indeed Morgan sitting on the bench. With a playful desire to surprise him, she quickly got dressed and quietly made her way to the back of the bench where he was working on his laptop.

She couldn't resist the temptation to read what he had been typing. To her amazement, she discovered that Morgan was preparing his final report, and his name was followed by 'M. S.' in Computer Science.

Filled with excitement and joy, she decided to reveal herself and share in his accomplishment. Sunayana appeared before him, surprising Morgan. With a warm smile, she said, "So this is the reality; this is you, Mr. Morgan Shaw. Why did you hide it from me? I had already guessed when we first met that you weren't just an ordinary cab driver. You're a Master of Science in computer technology. I am pleasantly surprised!"

Morgan was taken aback by her sudden appearance and her swift revelation of his educational background. He felt a bit embarrassed but quickly explained, "Oh, I'm sorry. Yes, it's me. I thought I would tell you once I have the result of this final report. My Head of Department is convinced that this project of mine will truly change my life."

As Sunayana sat beside Morgan on the bench, she expressed her confidence in his success, acknowledging that his Head of Department was right about the potential of his project. Playfully, she inquired if there were any more surprises he had in store for her.

Morgan responded warmly, "If you agree, we can be good friends."

With a smile, Sunayana affirmed, "Of course, we are good friends now."

Sunayana then shared that she was praying for his project's success, as Morgan was submitting it that day. She mentioned that she was currently pursuing her first year of M.B.A., making him her senior in the academic journey.

Morgan's smile widened as he said, "Now I will have to buy my own car. The other day you mentioned wanting to learn how to drive. I'll be happy to teach you in my own car."

Sunayana's excitement soared, and she eagerly exclaimed, "Really, Morgan? Will you teach me how to drive?"

Morgan playfully responded, "You are my friend now. I can do at least that much for the present, Sunayana."

Sunayana then made a small request, asking Morgan not to call her 'madam' since he was her senior. Instead, she requested him to simply call her 'Sunayana,' reinforcing their newfound friendship with a radiant smile.

Chapter 4

Increasing Proximity

Sunayana had a wonderful three days spent with Raman, Meeta, and their little daughter, creating beautiful memories together as they visited various places and enjoyed each other's company. However, the break came to an end, and she returned to her apartment on Sunday evening, preparing herself for the upcoming college week.

The following Monday, as she looked out of her window, she was taken aback by a pleasant surprise. In place of the familiar yellow cab, she saw a brand new white car parked on the road below. Her excitement soared as she noticed Morgan standing beside the car, holding a red flower.

Rushing downstairs, Sunayana greeted him warmly, but before she could express her gratitude, he shared the amazing news, "My dream has come true, Sunayana. Now I have become a lecturer in my department. My project is going to be displayed at an International Seminar this month. However, it's just the beginning; I have to go very far..."

Sunayana was elated for her friend and immediately congratulated him on his achievements. However, she couldn't help but notice a newfound maturity and prestige in Morgan's demeanor. His hard work and dedication had paid off, and his success was evident in the gleaming car before them and the accomplishments he had already achieved.

It was a proud moment for Sunayana to witness her friend's growth and the realization of his dreams.

As Morgan poured his heart out, Sunayana listened attentively, touched by the impact of their initial meeting and how she had unknowingly become an inspiration for him. His hard work and determination were a direct result of the motivation he drew from her words of encouragement.

Seeing tears welling up in his eyes, Sunayana gently placed her hand on his shoulder, offering comfort and support. Morgan quickly explained, "No, I'm not weeping because I have achieved less in life.

It's just that sometimes, I wish I had parents too."

His words conveyed a deep sense of longing, reminding Sunayana of the challenges he had faced in life, growing up in a Christian orphanage without the presence of biological parents.

She empathized with the void he must feel at times and admired his strength and resilience in overcoming adversities and achieving success.

As Sunayana looked into Morgan's face, her heart filled with compassion and understanding. She realized that he had never shared the details of his family background with her before. Curious and wanting to know more about his past, she gently asked, "You never told me about your parents. Have you ever seen them?"

Morgan's expression softened as he began to share his poignant story, "I am the son of a broken family. My father was a black African from Nigeria, and my mother was a white woman from America. They lived together as husband and wife for nine years, but one day, they left me alone and went away. I don't know where they are now. I waited for them in our house, crying for two days, but they never returned. On the third day, the Father from the local church found me in that house and took me with him."

Sunayana listened attentively, touched by the depth of pain and abandonment Morgan had experienced at such a young age. His story revealed the complexity of his background and the challenges he had faced growing up without the presence of his parents. She could only imagine the mix of emotions he must have carried throughout his life.

In that moment, Sunayana realized the strength of Morgan's character and his resilience in overcoming such adversity. He had risen above his difficult past, determined to pursue education and create a better future for himself. His achievements and the person he had become were a testament to his unwavering spirit.

As Sunayana expressed her admiration for Morgan's courage and resilience, he appreciated her kind words, feeling a deep sense of gratitude for her understanding and support. Their bond had grown even stronger, and Sunayana's compassion and companionship had a profound impact on Morgan's heart.

On that particular day, Sunayana decided to skip college to spend time with Morgan at his request. They made the most of the day, exploring the city together in his new car.

They visited various places, immersing themselves in the joy of each other's company. From the local zoo to the botanical garden, and then to the museum, they shared laughter and excitement, creating beautiful memories together.

They later had a delightful lunch at a posh restaurant, cherishing the moments they spent together. Morgan insisted that Sunayana join him for dinner in the evening, and after some initial hesitation, she agreed. Throughout the day, they enjoyed each other's company, and their friendship blossomed into something truly special.

Over the course of the next ten days, Sunayana and Morgan continued to spend time together, commuting to college in his new car and sharing pleasant evenings as they returned home. Their friendship had grown stronger, and they felt comfortable in each other's presence.

Sunayana's studies were progressing well, and she was excelling in her college work. Meanwhile, Morgan had also made a positive impact in his role as a lecturer in the Computer Department, becoming popular among his students.

As promised, Morgan had begun teaching Sunayana how to drive. Every time they sat together in the car, Sunayana felt a rush of excitement, her hands touching his on the steering wheel.

Being close to a man in this manner was a new experience for her, but she felt at ease in Morgan's company. He was patient and encouraging during the driving lessons, creating a safe and comfortable environment for her to learn.

Sunayana cherished the companionship they shared, and her heart was filled with admiration for Morgan. Their friendship had evolved into something special, and she appreciated the moments they spent together, whether it was having tea and snacks at her apartment or exploring the city in the car.

Sunayana was taken aback by the sweet surprise Morgan had prepared for her. As they arrived at the beautiful restaurant, she couldn't help but wonder why he had chosen this particular place. She playfully asked if it was his birthday, trying to find a reason for the unexpected celebration.

However, Morgan quickly revealed that birthdays didn't hold much significance for him, being an orphan. But he emphasized that having Sunayana by his side on that day brought him immense joy and delight.

With a warm smile, Morgan guided her into the restaurant, where they found a table for two already reserved. The atmosphere was enchanting, with a singer serenading the crowd with melodious tunes. The romantic ambiance made the surprise even more special, and Sunayana felt deeply touched by Morgan's thoughtful gesture.

As Sunayana noticed their names adorning one of the tables, her curiosity grew, and she playfully asked Morgan about the reason for this surprise. His response was heartfelt and genuine, as he shared the news of receiving his first salary and the desire to share his happiness with her.

Sunayana felt deeply touched by Morgan's openness and the trust he placed in their friendship. She encouraged him to celebrate his achievements and reminded him of his success, urging him to focus on the bright future ahead.

Gracing him with a gentle smile, she expressed her admiration, "Morgan, you should truly take pride in your accomplishments. Your success speaks volumes, a testament to your unwavering determination that has brought your dreams to fruition. Remember, your past doesn't define you; what truly counts is the person you are today and the bright future ahead of you."

Morgan agreed, acknowledging the wisdom in Sunayana's words. He realized that dwelling on his past wouldn't serve him well, and he needed to embrace the positive changes that had taken place in his life.

In a lighthearted manner, Morgan shifted the conversation toward the evening's culinary delights, asking Sunayana about her preferences for dinner. They immersed themselves in the joy of the present moment, savoring the delicious food and the wonderful atmosphere of the restaurant.

Sunayana glanced towards the adjacent table, where two young Indian men were savoring their drinks. Their attention was fixated on Sunayana and Morgan, and it appeared that one of them might have been intoxicated.

Sunayana had already discerned from their demeanor that their intentions were questionable. One of the men boldly addressed her, saying, "What's a girl like you doing with a cab driver? This restaurant is for the well-dressed crowd like us. Come and join us; you don't belong there."

As the situation escalated, the second man attempted to pull Sunayana forcefully, prompting Morgan to intervene and place himself between them.

The aggressor then struck Morgan on the back, but Morgan remained composed and did not retaliate. However, things took a turn for the worse when the man holding Sunayana's hand delivered a punch to Morgan's face, causing a drop of blood to trickle from his nose.

Sunayana gasped in fear, pulling her hand away from the man's grip. Witnesses at nearby tables noticed the commotion and rushed to intervene, attempting to diffuse the confrontation and restore order.

Suddenly, the situation took a dire turn as Morgan collapsed and lost consciousness. Concerned bystanders rushed to his aid, lifting him carefully and transporting him to a nearby hospital. Sunayana, visibly distressed and with tears in her eyes, accompanied him to the medical facility.

At the hospital, doctors attended to Morgan's injuries. They discovered a deep cut on the right side of his nose, likely caused by the ring the aggressive young man wore during the altercation. The medical team worked diligently to address and treat the wound, ensuring Morgan received the necessary care.

Sunayana remained at his side, anxiously awaiting news of his condition, her emotions running high with worry and concern.

"I'm sorry, Sunayana. I spoiled your evening. You see how my luck is! I am not allowed to share my happiness with anyone. Are you all right, Sunayana?" said Morgan, looking in her eyes.

"Thank God, Morgan, you are not seriously hurt. I am so relieved to see you all right. Those thugs could have further harmed you," said Sunayana very timidly, her voice tinged with genuine concern.

Throughout the night, Sunayana sat vigilantly beside Morgan's bed, refusing to sleep. She held his hand tightly, watching over him as he peacefully slept.

Her heart overflowed with affection and profound respect for him, sensing his loneliness and vulnerability. In that moment, Sunayana felt an unbreakable connection to him, as if he held a special place in her heart.

When morning came, Morgan was discharged from the hospital, but he insisted on going home. However, Sunayana was determined to take care of him, so she brought him to her apartment instead.

With the college closed for the day, they had the freedom to spend time together. Sunayana lovingly prepared breakfast for him and gently washed his face with warm water, taking care of his needs. She also tended to his wound, changing the bandage and ensuring he took the prescribed medication.

Sunayana's actions reflected her deep concern and affection for Morgan. She felt a strong sense of responsibility towards him and was determined to support him throughout his recovery. Their bond had grown even stronger through this ordeal, and Sunayana's devotion to her dear friend shone brightly in the tenderness of her care.

Morgan gazed at Sunayana and playfully remarked, "I wish I could get hurt from time to time, just so you could take care of me."

Sunayana smiled and replied in a teasing tone, "Oh, you're impossible! Don't even think about getting hurt again. And if you keep wishing for such things, I'll have no choice but to send you back to your home!"

As they bantered with each other, it became evident that they had grown fond of their newfound closeness. The genuine care and concern they had for one another brought them joy, and they cherished the special bond they had formed. Their hearts were drawn together, and they both cherished the presence of the other in their lives.

Sunayana cooked a delicious lunch for Morgan, and she happily taught him how to eat rotis with his hands, a traditional Indian way of eating. He thoroughly enjoyed the meal, savoring every bite.

Sunayana felt a sense of fulfillment seeing how much progress Morgan had made with his Hindi over the past three weeks. He had diligently learned hundreds of words and always used them with precision, putting effort into perfecting his accent.

During this time, Sunayana had come to realize that she felt whole and complete in Morgan's company, and he felt the same way. They had formed a deep connection that went beyond just friendship.

The bond they shared had grown stronger with each passing day, and they found solace and comfort in each other's presence. They both understood the value of their relationship and cherished the special moments they spent together.

As the days passed, Raman and his family were away in India for a month, but Sunayana never felt alone or abandoned. Morgan had become her constant companion and support.

They spent a lot of time together, and their connection grew stronger with each passing day. A tender affection seemed to be blossoming between them, hinting at the possibility of love.

Morgan's deep brown eyes had a mesmerizing effect on Sunayana, filling her with pleasant sensations whenever he looked at her. One day, Morgan expressed his feelings romantically, telling Sunayana that he never expected that someone like her would come into his life and add colors to his otherwise dull existence.

Feeling curious, Sunayana mustered the courage to ask Morgan about his past relationships. He candidly admitted that he had never had time to pursue love or relationships before. He had been focused on working hard to survive, which left little room for personal affairs. Meeting Sunayana seemed to coincide with his approaching success, and he found himself drawn to her.

Sunayana playfully teased him, saying that she wasn't immediately attracted to him, but Morgan dismissed it as a silly topic, diverting the conversation.

They continued to enjoy their coffee, cherishing each other's company and the bond they shared. As their relationship deepened, they found joy and contentment in each other, and the possibility of love seemed more promising than ever.

Morgan let out a sigh of relief upon hearing that Sunayana's condition was not serious. He held her hand tightly, feeling a mix of emotions inside him. He was relieved that she was safe, but the scare had made him realize just how much she meant to him.

Sunayana smiled at him, appreciating his concern and affection. His presence beside her brought a sense of comfort and reassurance. Morgan leaned over and kissed her palm tenderly, expressing his love and care for her.

The nurse observed their interaction and couldn't help but smile. She could see the strong bond between them, and she spoke kindly, acknowledging the love that Morgan had for Sunayana.

Feeling grateful and emotional, Morgan replied, "Yes, sister, she means the world to me. I never want to see her in pain or distress.

Today, I've come to realize how special she is to me."

The nurse reassured Morgan that Sunayana's condition was likely caused by exam stress, a common occurrence among students. Morgan felt grateful that it wasn't anything serious but resolved to be there for Sunayana, supporting and caring for her during this challenging time.

Chapter 5

Closeness & Domestic Joys

Sunayana felt overwhelmed by Morgan's care and affection for her. She couldn't deny the fact that she had become dependent on him, not just physically but emotionally as well. He had become her rock, her support, and her confidant.

As she recovered from her fainting spell, having Morgan by her side brought her immense relief and happiness. His presence seemed to erase all her worries and fears. He had become an integral part of her life, filling it with joy and companionship.

Morgan's words about Sunayana being his inspiration touched her deeply. She had never thought that she could have such a profound impact on someone's life. It made her realize the strength of their bond and how they had become each other's source of strength.

When Morgan drove her back to her apartment, he treated her with utmost care and delicacy, as if she were the most precious thing in the world. His gentle touch and concern made her heart swell with affection for him.

Once they reached her bedroom, he continued to be gentle and attentive, making sure she was comfortable before leaving. Sunayana felt blessed to have someone like

Morgan by her side, someone who cared for her so deeply and selflessly.

As she lay in bed, she couldn't help but think about how much Morgan meant to her. She had never imagined that she would find such a genuine connection with someone so far from her homeland.

Sunayana couldn't help but smile at Morgan's determination to take care of her. His concern and devotion touched her deeply. She appreciated his willingness to stay with her even though he had his own commitments and responsibilities.

In a caring tone, she reached out to him, "Morgan, there's no need for you to go to such great lengths. I can manage on my own. You have your class tomorrow, and you need some rest as well."

But Morgan was adamant. "I can't leave you alone, Sunayana. I don't mind sleeping on the floor. It's nothing for me. I want to be here to make sure you're okay."

Sunayana felt a mix of emotions - gratitude, affection, and a sense of protection that Morgan offered. She knew she couldn't persuade him to leave, so she decided to accept his caring gesture. After all, she had grown fond of his presence and didn't want to push him away.

"Okay, Morgan. If you insist, you can stay. But you don't have to sleep on the floor. We have a comfortable couch in the living room.

You can sleep there," she said, trying to compromise.

Morgan smiled warmly, appreciating her concern for his comfort. "That's very kind of you, Sunayana. I'll take the couch then. But if you need anything during the night, just call me. I'll be here."

Sunayana couldn't help but admire Morgan's unwavering determination to stay and take care of her. His selflessness and concern touched her heart deeply. She finished her coffee and placed the cup on the bedside table.

"Alright, Morgan. If you're determined to stay, I won't argue further. Thank you for being here," she said softly, a gentle smile gracing her face.

Morgan smiled back and closed his eyes, settling into his makeshift bed on the floor. Sunayana turned off the lights and lay down on the bed, pulling the blanket over herself. She couldn't help but feel grateful for having Morgan by her side, willing to sacrifice his own comfort for her well-being.

Sunayana's mind was filled with conflicting emotions as she lay there, gazing at Morgan. While she couldn't deny the deep affection she felt for him, she also knew that her traditional Indian parents might have reservations about her relationship with a man from a different culture and background.

She knew that her parents had certain expectations and traditions when it came to marriage. They might want her to marry someone from their own community or at least someone with a similar cultural background. The idea of introducing Morgan as a potential partner to her parents felt daunting and uncertain.

As she thought about her parents' reaction, Sunayana couldn't help but worry about the possible challenges and misunderstandings that might arise. She knew that their acceptance of Morgan would be a significant hurdle to overcome.

In the midst of her internal struggle, Sunayana glanced at Morgan again. He was sleeping peacefully, unaware of the turmoil in her mind. She admired his strength and resilience, but she also feared the potential complications their relationship might bring.

As the night wore on, Sunayana wrestled with her emotions and tried to imagine a future with Morgan. She didn't know what the future held, but for now, she cherished the bond they shared and the happiness he brought into her life.

The doorbell rang suddenly, causing Sunayana to startle. She wondered who could be at her door at this hour. As the doorbell rang for the second time, Morgan got up from the mattress and sat on it. Sunayana joined him, and fear was evident in her eyes.

Morgan assured her, "Don't be scared, my friend, I will go and see." He approached the door and opened it, revealing a man and a woman standing there with a suitcase.

Morgan asked, "Who are you looking for?"

The man replied firmly, "Sunayana, we have come to meet Sunayana. She lives here, doesn't she?"

Affirming the connection, Morgan replied, "Yes, she resides here, but unfortunately, she's unwell today. How do you happen to know her?" However, before he could get an answer, the man and woman entered the house.

Sunayana was fully awake now and exclaimed, "Father, Mother! You're here in America! Is everything okay?"

Her father's voice was firm and angry as he responded, "Nothing is okay! We believed you were here to study, but we have discovered what you're really doing. You have brought shame to our family. Are you not ashamed? You're staying with a stranger in your apartment."

"No, Papa, you have it all wrong. It's not like that. Morgan is a professor at our university. He took me to the hospital today, and he's here to help me," Sunayana tried to explain.

"Enough! We spoke with Raman in India, and he told us everything about you and this man. You, my daughter, are having an affair with this taxi driver. We have come here to take you back to India!" her father's eyes were filled with anger.

"I understand now. Raman gave you only part of the information and misled you. Let me clarify the situation for you. Morgan is currently a professor. Many students here work part-time jobs to support their education. Yes, he used to drive a taxi, but now he is a professor of Computer Science at our college," Sunayana explained in detail.

Morgan had been patient while listening, but he couldn't remain silent any longer, "Please try to stay calm. We haven't done anything wrong. We genuinely care for each other..."

Before Morgan could utter another word, Sunayana's father raised his voice, "Shut up and get out!"

Sunayana stood up and spoke to Morgan, "Please leave, Morgan. I can't bear to see you insulted here."

"But Sunayana, let me explain why I stayed here in your apartment," Morgan pleaded.

"They won't listen to anything right now. They are not in a state to understand. I will have to talk to them and convince them," Sunayana reassured him.

"I'll only leave under one condition: promise me that you won't let your parents emotionally manipulate you. Sunayana, I love you, and I want you to promise that you'll stay true to yourself. If you do that, I'll be right by your side," Morgan expressed earnestly, gazing deeply into her eyes.

"I promise! I am always here for you. Please go home. I can't bear to see you insulted," Sunayana replied.

With affection in his eyes, Morgan gazed at her face and turned away, slowly walking out of her apartment.

After Morgan's departure, Sunayana's parents started shouting at her, showing no signs of being impressed by her tears. They subjected her to verbal abuse, insisting that she gather her belongings and prepare to return to her home.

"I can't leave my studies. Please listen to me," Sunayana pleaded, tears streaming down her face.

"No, I will not listen to any excuse now. You do not need higher education," her father declared, unwavering in his decision.

Her mother joined in the shouting, expressing her displeasure at Sunayana's choice of partner. She berated her daughter for being in love with someone with unknown parentage.

"Mummy, please listen carefully! Morgan is not a taxi driver; he is a professor. And even if he were a taxi driver, he would still be respected in America. The most important thing is that we love each other, and we want to get married," Sunayana retorted loudly, displaying her defiance.

Her father continued to express his dismay, questioning how they could face society with such a match.

"No, Papa, I have no fear of speaking the truth. I am an adult, and you can't force me to do anything against my wishes. Morgan has faced many hardships in his life, but now he is a successful man. I can't leave him now. It is too late," Sunayana declared firmly, standing her ground.

"How dare you talk like that to your father and mother? Have we raised you to be so disrespectful?" her father threatened to hit her, but Sunayana bravely stopped his hand in mid-air.

"If I dial 911, the police will promptly apprehend you, Papa, and you may face imprisonment for threatening me. This is America, Papa, not India. Girls have their liberty here. They are not treated like slaves as they are in India," Sunayana retorted with passion, unable to hold back her emotions.

"Will you send your father to jail? Is this what you have learned in America? How will we face our relatives and society?" her mother reacted with disapproval, expressing her disdainful disapproval through a hateful glare.

"Mother, please try to understand the concept of ownership and freedom. I don't want to insult you, but parents should respect their daughter's life and choices. An adult girl has the right to choose her life partner. I will not accept the man you choose for me," Sunayana explained calmly.

"Do you think we are your enemies? After all, you are our daughter," her mother retorted angrily.

"I had forgotten that, Mummy. Uncle's daughter was married into a wealthy family, but they killed her by burning her because our uncle couldn't provide the dowry they demanded," Sunayana spoke with fury, exposing the grim reality of some traditional practices.

Her mother and father fell silent as Sunayana dialed Morgan's number.

"Are you truly serious about marrying me, Morgan? I need your answer by 7:00 am tomorrow. Take your time and carefully consider it," she urged, speaking hastily.

Morgan's response was swift and unwavering, "I can't wait until morning. If I marry anyone in this life, it will only be you. I have no interest in anyone else. I'm ready to marry you."

Her mind made up, Sunayana declared with determination, "Then let's get married at the local church tomorrow. We'll inform our friends and classmates. I'll be there at 9:00 am."

Her mother's anger flared up, "Are you out of your mind? In this country, people marry one day and get divorced the next. How can you trust a man whose own parents abandoned him?"

Sunayana stood her ground, asserting, "Yes, I trust him completely. He is like pure gold, and despite all the hardships he faced, I believe in him wholeheartedly."

Her father remained silent, seemingly starting to grasp the cultural differences between America and India.

He pondered deeply on Sunayana's words, recalling the tragic incident with his brother's daughter. It dawned on him that Sunayana was speaking the truth.

When Sunayana turned to look at her father, she spoke with sincerity, "I humbly request you to be present at our marriage and bless us. Without your blessings, our union will feel incomplete. Morgan is an exceptional man, a true gentleman. Humanity transcends religious and caste barriers, Father."

But her father remained skeptical and asked, "How can you be so sure that he won't leave you after some years?"

"Papa, Morgan is a self-made man, just like you. You've always admired and respected hardworking individuals. He is honest and sincere, and he never lies to me. I assure you, I will never make a wrong decision in my life," Sunayana said with conviction.

Her father looked into her eyes, and a soft smile appeared on his face, "You've always been a determined and strong-willed child. I suppose I have no choice but to trust your judgment..."

Overwhelmed with joy, Sunayana rushed into her father's arms, "Thank you, Papa! Thank you so much. Now I can proudly say that I have understanding parents, not any less than parents from rich and advanced countries."

Sunayana walked into the kitchen, her mind still in a pleasant shock from the sudden turn of events. It all happened so quickly, and she found it hard to believe. The courage she had shown to take this big decision amazed even herself.

She picked up her phone and called Morgan, "I'm preparing coffee for my parents. If you'd like to have one last coffee with your girlfriend's parents, you're welcome, because starting tomorrow, your wife will be the one serving you coffee."

About fifteen minutes later, Morgan walked into the apartment with a bouquet of flowers in his hands. He graciously handed the flowers to Sunayana's mother and touched her feet, seeking her blessings. He then did the same with Sunayana's father, showing his respect and seeking their approval.

Sunayana couldn't help but smile and said, "One more thing, Mummy and Papa, Morgan speaks Hindi."

Her parents were pleasantly surprised as Morgan began to converse with them in Hindi.

The rest of the night was filled with laughter and conversation. Everyone seemed to be happy and at ease. Sunayana's father had made countless phone calls to his relatives in India, informing them about the upcoming marriage.

He even proposed that after the wedding, both Sunayana and Morgan would visit India with them, and he would host a grand celebration at his bungalow in Delhi.

Joy and warmth filled Sunayana's little apartment that night.